BREAD AND CEREAL/PAN Y CEREALES

by/por Tea Benduhn

Reading consultant/Consultora de lectura: Susan Nations, M.Ed.,
author, literacy coach, consultant in literacy development/
autora, tutora de alfabetización, consultora de desarrollo de la lectura

WEEKLY READER®
PUBLISHING

Please visit our web site at: **www.garethstevens.com**
For a free color catalog describing our list of high-quality books,
call 1-800-542-2595 (USA) or 1-800-387-3178 (Canada).

Library of Congress Cataloging-in-Publication Data available upon request from publisher.

ISBN: 978-0-8368-8454-8 (lib. bdg.)
ISBN: 978-0-8368-8461-6 (softcover)

This edition first published in 2008 by
Weekly Reader® Books
An imprint of Gareth Stevens Publishing
1 Reader's Digest Road
Pleasantville, NY 10570-7000 USA

Copyright © 2008 by Gareth Stevens, Inc.

Managing editor: Valerie J. Weber
Art direction: Tammy West
Graphic designer: Scott Krall
Picture research: Diane Laska-Swanke
Photographer: Gregg Andersen
Production: Jessica Yanke
Spanish translation: Tatiana Acosta and Guillermo Gutiérrez

Printed in the United States of America

1 2 3 4 5 6 7 8 9 11 10 09 08 07

Note to Educators and Parents

Reading is such an exciting adventure for young children! They are beginning to integrate their oral language skills with written language. To encourage children along the path to early literacy, books must be colorful, engaging, and interesting; they should invite the young reader to explore both the print and the pictures.

The *Find Out About Food* series is designed to help children understand the value of good nutrition and eating to stay healthy. In each book, young readers will learn how their favorite foods — and possibly some new ones — fit into a balanced diet.

Each book is specially designed to support the young reader in the reading process. The familiar topics are appealing to young children and invite them to read — and re-read — again and again. The full-color photographs and enhanced text further support the student during the reading process.

In addition to serving as wonderful picture books in schools, libraries, homes, and other places where children learn to love reading, these books are specifically intended to be read within an instructional guided reading group. This small group setting allows beginning readers to work with a fluent adult model as they make meaning from the text. After children develop fluency with the text and content, the book can be read independently. Children and adults alike will find these books supportive, engaging, and fun!

— Susan Nations, M.Ed., author, literacy coach, and consultant in literacy development

Nota para los maestros y los padres

¡Leer es una aventura tan emocionante para los niños pequeños! A esta edad están comenzando a integrar su manejo del lenguaje oral con el lenguaje escrito. Para animar a los niños en el camino de la lectura incipiente, los libros deben ser coloridos, estimulantes e interesantes; deben invitar a los jóvenes lectores a explorar la letra impresa y las ilustraciones.

Conoce la comida es una colección diseñada para ayudar a los jóvenes lectores a entender la importancia de una nutrición apropiada y el papel de la alimentación en la salud. En cada libro, los jóvenes lectores aprenderán de qué forma sus alimentos favoritos —y posiblemente algunos nuevos— pueden formar parte de una dieta balanceada.

Cada libro está especialmente diseñado para ayudar a los jóvenes lectores en el proceso de lectura. Los temas familiares llaman la atención de los niños y los invitan a leer una y otra vez. Las fotografías a todo color y el tamaño de la letra ayudan aún más al estudiante en el proceso de lectura.

Además de servir como maravillosos libros ilustrados en escuelas, bibliotecas, hogares y otros lugares donde los niños aprenden a amar la lectura, estos libros han sido especialmente concebidos para ser leídos en un grupo de lectura guiada. Este contexto permite que los lectores incipientes trabajen con un adulto que domina la lectura mientras van determinando el significado del texto. Una vez que los niños dominan el texto y el contenido, el libro puede ser leído de manera independiente. ¡Estos libros les resultarán útiles, estimulantes y divertidos a niños y a adultos por igual!

— Susan Nations, M.Ed., autora, tutora de alfabetización, consultora de desarrollo de la lectura

Do you like to eat oatmeal for breakfast? Oatmeal is made out of oats. Oats are **cereal grains**.

¿Te gusta desayunar copos de avena? Los copos de avena son **granos de cereal**.

Cereal grains are foods that come from plants. Wheat and rice are grains. Popcorn is a grain, too!

Los granos de cereal son alimentos que vienen de las plantas. El trigo y el arroz son granos. ¡El maíz con el que se hacen las palomitas también es un tipo de grano!

Grains are part of the **food pyramid**. The six colored bands on the food pyramid stand for types of foods. Make smart choices. Eat these foods and **exercise** every day.

Los granos son parte de la **pirámide alimentaria**. Cada una de las seis franjas de colores de la pirámide representa un tipo de alimento. Elige de forma inteligente. Consume estos alimentos y haz **ejercicio** todos los días.

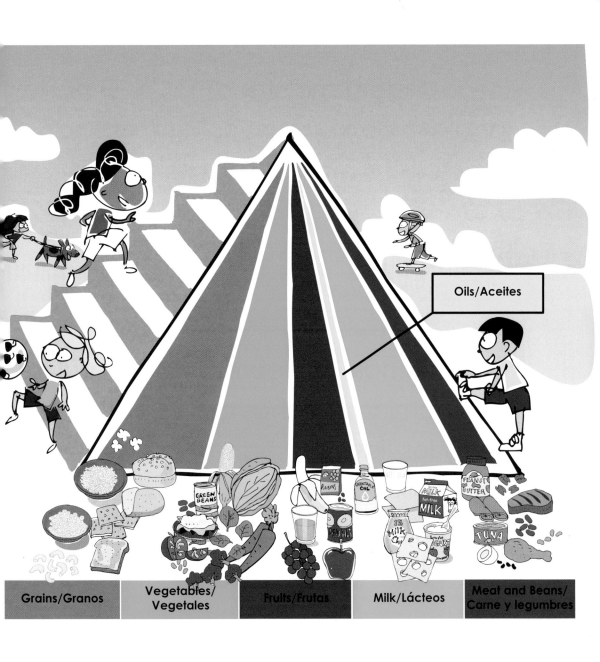

Oils/Aceites

Grains/Granos

Vegetables/
Vegetales

Fruits/Frutas

Milk/Lácteos

Meat and Beans/
Carne y legumbres

The orange band stands for grains and foods made from grains. Bread and noodles are made from grains. It is the widest band. Every day, you should eat more grains than any other food group.

La franja naranja representa los granos y las comidas hechas con granos. El pan y los fideos se hacen con granos. Esta franja es la más ancha. A diario, debes comer más cereales que cualquier otra clase de alimentos.

11

What other kinds of grains do you eat? Do you eat crackers, pretzels, or bread? All of these foods are made from grains.

¿Qué otra clase de granos comes? ¿Comes galletas, *pretzels* o pan? Todos esos alimentos se hacen con granos.

13

Grains are good for you to eat.
They help your heart stay **healthy**.

Comer granos es bueno. Los
granos te ayudan a tener un
corazón **saludable**.

15

Grains build strong bones. They also help you run and play. Grains even help you go to the bathroom!

Los granos te permiten tener huesos fuertes. También te ayudan a jugar y correr. ¡Los granos te ayudan incluso a ir al baño!

Some kinds of grains are better for you than others. **Whole grains** are the best. Bread made from whole wheat tastes good, too!

Algunos tipos de granos son mejores para ti que otros. Los **granos integrales** son los mejores. ¡El pan hecho con harina de trigo integral también sabe rico!

How can you eat enough whole grains? Pancakes can be made with whole wheat. You can even eat whole wheat muffins!

¿Qué puedes hacer para comer suficientes granos integrales? Se pueden preparar panquecas con harina integral. ¡Hasta te puedes comer un *muffin* de harina integral!

Glossary/Glosario

food pyramid — the drawing that shows six colored bands that stand for the six different food groups people should eat every day

grains — cereal plants, such as wheat, corn, and oats

healthy — strong and free from illness

whole grains — the inside and the outside of grain kernels, or seeds

- -

granos — semillas de las plantas de cereal como el trigo, el maíz y la avena

granos integrales — semillas de los cereales que conservan su capa exterior

pirámide alimentaria — dibujo que muestra seis franjas de colores que representan seis grupos diferentes de alimentos que las personas deben comer a diario

saludable — fuerte y sin enfermedades

For More Information/Más información

Books/Libros

The Grain Group. Healthy Eating with MyPyramid (series). Mari C. Schuh (Capstone Press)

Grains. Blastoff! Readers: The New Food Guide Pyramid (series). Emily K. Green (Scholastic)

Los cereales. Los grupos de alimentos (series). Robin Nelson (Lerner Publications)

Web Sites/Páginas Web

My Pyramid for Kids

mypyramid.gov/kids/index.html
Click on links to play a game and learn more at the government's Web site about the food pyramid.

Publisher's note to educators and parents: Our editors have carefully reviewed this Web site to ensure that it is suitable for children. Many Web sites change frequently, however, and we cannot guarantee that a site's future contents will continue to meet our high standards of quality and educational value. Be advised that children should be closely supervised whenever they access the Internet.

Index/Índice

About the Author/Información sobre la autora

Tea Benduhn writes and edits books for children and teens. She lives in the beautiful state of Wisconsin with her husband and two cats. The walls of their home are lined with bookshelves filled with books. Tea says, "I read every day. It is more fun than watching television!"

Tea Benduhn escribe y corrige libros para niños y adolescentes. Vive en el bello estado de Wisconsin con su esposo y dos gatos. Las paredes de su casa están cubiertas de estanterías con libros. Tea dice: "Leo todos los días. ¡Es más divertido que ver televisión!".